Curious George®

AND THE DUMP TRUCK

pc

Adapted from the Curious George film series
Edited by Margret Rey and Alan J. Shalleck

1 9 8 4

Houghton Mifflin Company Boston

Library of Congress Cataloging in Publication Data
Main entry under title:

Curious George and the dump truck.

"Adapted from the Curious George film series, edited
by Margret Rey and Alan J. Shalleck."
Summary: Curious George gets into trouble when he
boards a dump truck and spills a load of sand in the road
but redeems himself when the sand blocks the getaway of
jewelry thieves.
1. Children's stories, American. [1. Monkeys—
Fiction. 2. Robbers and outlaws—Fiction] I. Rey,
Margret. II. Shalleck, Alan J. III. Curious George and
the dump truck (Motion picture)
PZ7.C92   1984   [E]   84-16824
ISBN 0-395-36635-6 (lib. bdg.)
ISBN 0-395-36629-1 (pbk.)

Printed in Japan

10 9 8 7 6 5 4 3 2 1

"I have to go to town, George," said the man
with the yellow hat. "You can come along."

George and his friend got into their blue car
and drove to town.

On the way, they listened to the news on the radio.

"There has been a robbery at Gilbert's Jewelry Store,"
the announcer said. "The robbers were seen driving
away in a red van."

"George," said the man. "I have to buy some nails. Wait for me in the car, but don't get into trouble."

Some workmen with a big dump truck were fixing the
holes in the street.

At noontime, the men stopped for lunch.

George got out of the car and climbed into the truck.

He was curious. What were all those levers?
He pulled one after the other.

Suddenly, the truck began to dump.

It dumped sand all over the street. The sand
spilled over a lady in a flowered hat.

It spilled over a man with an umbrella.

The people were angry. "What's going on?"
they cried. "Who's dumping all that sand?"

When the workmen returned from lunch, they saw
the mess. "Grab that monkey," one of them shouted.

George was scared. Quickly, he ran up a telephone
pole.

No one could reach him there.

The workmen began to shovel the sand back
into the truck.

Just then, a red van came around the corner.
George heard a police car siren.

The police must be chasing someone. Maybe they were chasing George.

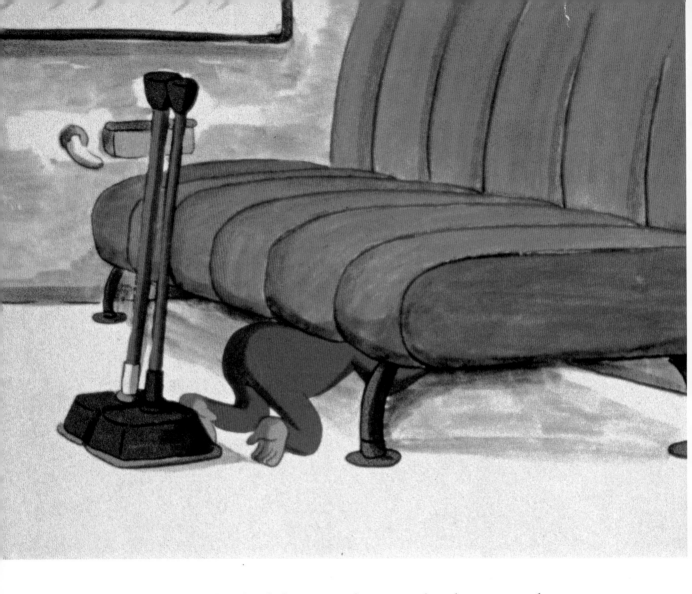

He climbed down and ran to the dump truck.

He tried to crawl under the seat but his foot hit
the dumping lever again.

All of the sand was dumped!

The sandpile got so high that it blocked the road.

George covered his head and waited for the police to
take him away. But the police were not after George.

They wanted the men in the red van who had
robbed the jewelry store.

The police caught the robbers and took them away.

Now George came out of his hiding place.

"You were a bad monkey," one of the workmen said.
"Hold it," said the policeman, "he helped us catch
the robbers."

"You're right," said the workman.
"You're okay, George. Let's shake hands."

That night they were watching TV.
"A little monkey saved the day," the 6:00 P.M. news
report began …

9513 46